Crying Over Flowers

Frozen Moon

Crying Over Flowers

Cover Design: Enchanted Ink Publishing
Editing: A.E. Williams, Louise Pearce
Book Design and Typesetting: Enchanted Ink Publishing

The text type was set in Lora

ISBN: 978-1-7394561-3-9 (E-book)
ISBN: 978-1-7394561-4-6 (Paperback)

Thank you for your support of the author's rights.

W W W . F R O Z E N M O O N P R E S S . C O M

Frozen Moon

For all the Nodos, Hadis, and Alinas.

May you find comfort within these pages.

Crying Over Flowers

BEN T. CLARKE

Chapter 1
27

'M NODO. FOR THE LAST MONTH, I'VE BEEN TWENTY-SEVEN. Time was passing so quickly that I struggled to catch my breath. Sometimes I worried I hadn't accomplished enough for my age. *Twenty-seven is so young. You still have your whole life ahead of you,* they said.

My twenty-two-year-old self had thought that I'd be crowded with friends at twenty-seven, have a colourful social life, no stress, a hot girlfriend, a great job, and pursuing all my passions unrelentingly. It felt like just yesterday I was twenty-two.

I guess I shouldn't complain too much. I had a solid job, and a few years ago, I moved into my shoebox apartment away from my parents' house. I liked art, galleries, quiet coffee shops, and pretty flowers. When I was younger, I dreamed of becoming a famous artist and having my art in galleries. My biggest concern was which pencil I should use. I was such a naive child.

Would I have called myself happy? Maybe *comfortable* would have fit better. After all, what was happiness? I only caught glimpses of it as it flashed before my eyes and vanished. It would leave me amazed as if that feeling was a luxury I didn't deserve. Maybe I'm not qualified to say whether I was happy or not. I never experienced enough of it to explain what it felt like.

I liked my job. A small, independent bistro-style restaurant with fifteen staff. Eight in the kitchen, three on the bar, and four servers. I recently got a promotion to lead the front of house. It came with a small pay rise and triple the responsibility. I often questioned whether the pay was worth it. It wasn't much money, but even the smallest amount meant less stress outside of work. The responsibility was the worst thing about the job. I didn't care what the front-of-house team did as long as it wouldn't get me in trouble. If they were good, I was good; if I was good, then the boss was great. Sometimes, it felt like my entire life's purpose was to work in a small restaurant, serving above-average food and earning a few pounds over minimum wage. I took a sliver of joy in recommending dishes, pairing wines with meals, and telling customers which desserts were my personal favourites. When I was inside the restaurant, it felt like that was my entire world, that nothing outside of that tiny little building mattered. As long as things were done right and customers left happy, everything would be okay. Perhaps that was why I had stayed there for seven years, working six days a week, and, of course, the free food kept me from quitting.

In the kitchen was Hadi. He was the closest thing I could've called a friend. He was a year older than me, with dark skin, fluffy brown hair, a well-built figure, and a wonderful sense of humour. An indelible smile was always painted on his face. For a chef, he was far too joyful. Half the kitchen staff would have quit if it weren't for him. Not a bad word about him was ever whispered behind closed doors.

At first, I had only viewed Hadi as a coworker. It wasn't until he began to invite me out for drinks after the closing shift that I saw potential in making him a friend. He was the first person to invite me out. He was the same inside and outside of work. However, when it was just the two of us, he spoke more truthfully and passionately, as if he wasn't ashamed of anything in front of me.

I never felt I could speak as rawly as him. I could tell he wished for me to express my deepest thoughts, but I didn't, even though I'd known him for six years since he joined the kitchen as a bubbly, enthusiastic chef.

I had no reason to dislike him and every reason to like him. He was kind, happy, truthful, everything good you could say about a man. I enjoyed his company, but sometimes, I couldn't shake the feeling he was holding up a facade. Nobody was truly that happy, that carefree. It made me feel distant from him.

Chapter 2
TUESDAYS

PLACED THE LAST CHAIR ON THE TABLE, ITS WOODEN SPLINTERS tickling my fingers. The restaurant closed at half past ten, with the last order being at ten. After all the closing duties were finished, we'd often get out anytime between eleven and one.

The restaurant's dark interior, with dark wood and candles on each table, was elegant and made one feel at peace. Behind the bar was a wine shelf with over two hundred bottles of various wines. It took me two years to learn all the wine jargon customers often spouted. Even so, they used words that I had never heard.

'Hey,' Alina said, trailing out the word like honey on her tongue. 'I've finished behind the bar. It's okay if I clock out now?'

Alina was the head bartender, as we called her. Twenty-six years she had lived for, but she smiled like a child. Pure, with no ulterior motive. Her black hair ended just above her shoulders, often wavy. Sometimes she'd wear these black, thick-rimmed glasses, but only when she didn't have time or had forgotten to put in her contact lenses. After coming to work, whilst she cut limes and I polished glasses, I'd listen to her complaints about forgetting her contacts.

'Sure. See you tomorrow?'

'Yeah. But I finish at seven.'

She and Hadi were perhaps the only people I enjoyed working with. Her happiness felt natural. And her anger, grumpiness, and tiredness all seemed to come naturally to her. She was awfully real. And I liked that. Human, unlike so many humans who didn't know how to behave as one. Like myself.

The rest of my coworkers existed, but they injected me with no happiness, sadness, or any other emotion. They were there, and that was the end of it. Most people were like that in my life. Evoking no emotions within me. Sometimes I found people funny; sometimes I laughed; sometimes they pissed me off; sometimes I admired them, or respected them, but even these emotions were fleeting. Then they'd go back to being zombies. Existing like a pencil on my desk. Sometimes that pencil was sharp and sketched so well, but it was only a brief experience of joy. Other times it was blunt and didn't draw the line I wanted. Even that was a momentary moment of annoyance.

It was rare for me to find people emotionally interesting, yet I often found myself staring at strangers, thinking about their lives.

I walked to the back to grab a brush, and Alina followed behind me on the way to clock out.

'By the way.' Her tone of voice shifted, becoming shaky. 'Are you working next Tuesday?'

'Nah, no work. Lucky me, right.' I threw in a smile.

I always had Tuesdays off, and I worked every other day. She knew this, so why did she ask?

'Me neither,' she said, her eyes becoming jumpy. 'You got any plans?'

'I want to go to an art gallery. I found this small one, actually. It's quite close to here, 'bout a twenty-minute walk.' I felt myself smiling. 'It looks great. It's on the second floor of this random building. Kinda hidden. Maybe that's why I've never noticed it.'

'That's right, you like art.' Her eyes drifted to the floor. 'I like art, too.'

My heart skipped a beat, and I felt a lump push its way into my throat. A stone trying to escape. 'Well, if you're not doing anything. Maybe you wanna come with me? Only if you have time, of course—'

'Yes. I'll go! Tuesday, right? Okay, I'll message you.'

She clocked out, then left, waving before she pushed through the door. I stood there for a second. Now only Hadi and I remained in the store. He was in the kitchen, finishing the cleaning.

Was this excitement? Was I becoming sick? I couldn't tell. But my stomach churned. Holy shit. Was I going on a date? Without thinking, I ran into the kitchen, sliding through the double doors.

'I asked her out!'

Hadi was polishing one of the stainless-steel pans with precision when I came in. But he dropped it onto the stone floor within an instant, sending a loud *clatter* through the air. 'Shut up! With Alina?'

'Yes!'

Laughs erupted from his mouth. He ran over and wrapped an arm around me, making my legs buckle slightly. ''Bout time! What happened? Tell me everything!'

He released me and sat on the counter, swinging his legs like a kid. 'Come on, Nodo! What happened.'

I took a breath, gathering my thoughts. The kitchen smelled of chemical cleaners and floral soap. Leaning against the metal counter, I recalled everything, down to the last word. As I recalled the story, I felt no shame in what I said. Excitement oozed out of me; I didn't have time to worry about anything else.

'Wait, so did you ask her out, or did she ask you out? Coz that was some heavy hinting,' he teased.

'Well, it was mutual, I guess.'

But now that I had finished retelling the story, the excitement faded. I realised I had never called it a date. Was it a date? Or were two friends going to a gallery? Maybe not even friends – two coworkers hanging out on their day off. Did that fit better?

'I never said it was a date.' My smile faded.

'What?' Hadi's smile got even bigger as if he'd stolen mine. 'Of course, it's a date! She *likes* you, bro! It's taken you long enough to realise it.'

'Really? You think she likes me?'

The thought seemed ridiculous to me. Why would anyone like me? I was extraordinarily ordinary. I was as plain as it gets. Even I wouldn't like myself. Liking me was like liking a plain piece of paper.

'Man, listen.' Hadi leant forward, his hands clutching the sides of the counter. 'This woman *wants* you.' He giggled. 'Wanna know something funny? Last night, I spoke to Ri about this. Literally last night. We both don't understand why you haven't made a move yet.' He giggled again. 'It's like we manifested this. You're welcome.'

Ri was his fiancée. They got engaged a few months ago and have been together for about five years. It felt like everyone my age was getting married, having kids, and settling down. But I was only twenty-seven. I was still young, right? I still had my whole life ahead of me.

'It's not that easy.' I felt myself smiling in an attempt to cover my awkwardness. 'Anyway, I guess we're going on a date now. So it doesn't matter how long it took.'

Hadi jumped off the counter. 'That's my boy. Wanna get a drink? We'll run through the plan – where you gonna go, what you gonna do. Man, I'm excited for you!'

We clocked out and left. I never ended up sweeping the floor.

We went to the nearest pub and ordered two beers. Until two in the morning, we talked about what I'd do.

Was this one of those fleeting moments of happiness? If it was, I never wanted it to end.

Chapter 3
COFFEE

I SAID I HAD ONLY VIEWED HADI AS A COWORKER OR SOMETHING along those lines. But now that I think about it more, he was the best friend I'd ever had. Maybe that wasn't hard, because he was my only friend. I wish I could've spoken more deeply to him. I wish I could've told him all my fears without a shred of fear. I wish I could have talked to him like he talked to me.

Hadi was confident, energetic, and happy, which, I guess, scared me a bit. When I was with him, I felt good. What I didn't like was how different he felt from me. How could he be so great, but not me? Perhaps I was jealous.

My life had been average. There was no better word for it. I'd had an average childhood with average hobbies and achievements. It was bland. Even my looks were average: brown hair, a slender build, and average height. I wanted some form of excitement in my life; I wanted to be like Hadi.

I did have art and painting. They were the only things that made me want to pursue this dull life.

We were in the pub after work, as usual. We sat at a booth, just the two of us. It was loud, as always, on a Monday night.

Cigarette smoke drifted through the open door, mixed with the smell of alcohol and greasy food, creating an almost nostalgic smell.

Hadi was on his fourth beer, whilst I was still on my first. It was impressive that no matter how much he drank, he never appeared to be drunk in the slightest. He always kept a level head and never made a fool of himself. I doubted he was the kind of guy to lie awake the next morning, eating himself up about something he might have done drunk.

'Run over your plan, one last time.' He leant towards me with his head in his hand. 'The first date is *the* most important. It's gonna determine whether you get a second one or not.'

I explained every detail, mapping it out with my hand on the sticky table. It felt *safe*, like nothing could go wrong – perfect.

At the end of our plan, Hadi laughed. He downed the rest of his beer and stood. 'Proud of you, my boy. Sleep well tonight.'

I nodded as we walked out of the bar through the groups of rowdy people.

'Nervous?'

'Just a little.'

'Bro, you're a catch. If I weren't gettin' married, I'd take you out on a date myself.'

'I thought we're on a date right now.' I smiled at my joke.

He laughed even harder and slapped me on the back.

Hot water was one of my favourite things. How was it possible that all I had to do was turn a little silver knob, and I could have an endless stream of refreshing, cleansing hot water? It was one of the few things that brought me to the brink of tears. I wasn't sure why. When it flowed over my naked body, I felt as though a god were caressing me. It made me feel clean.

After sleeping, I always woke up feeling disgusting. Every part of me felt vile. It made me sick. My skin felt tight, yet droopy. My limbs ached. My mouth felt dry and disgusting. I was sure I stank in the mornings before a shower, like an awful smell that would send someone into a coma or maybe wake someone from one. I saved having a shower until the last possible moment before I left the apartment. After a shower, I felt cleansed, and I wanted that feeling to last as long as possible. Why would I waste it being alone?

I shaved, took a dump, brushed my teeth, and finally showered.

Jeans, a top, and a navy-blue sweater. I'd never had a good sense of style. I wore what looked good and was casual. I figured that would be the best idea to wear today, too. Keep it comfortable, but smart, Hadi had said.

Before I left, I looked in the mirror. For a second, I thought I looked good. But then I smiled. I smiled, and then instantly stopped. It was wretched. Disgusting. Like ugly wrinkles pulling at my skin in rancid ways. Sickness overtook me. Now my hair didn't look good. With my hands, I brushed it down, forcing the rusty brown-coloured wires to stay in place.

I swallowed the spit that accumulated in my mouth, like gulping water. I decided to brush my teeth one last time before leaving.

I wasn't improving, so I pulled on my black trainers and left. Never had I been overly conscious of my looks; it wasn't that I thought I looked bad. It was just that I could have looked so much better. I was ashamed of my body. I didn't work out, but I ate healthily, yet I had hardly any muscles. I wanted to work out, but after work, I was always too tired, so I never felt like it. The mornings were the only time I could indulge in art, so that's what I did. Often, I found that if I looked too long at my reflection, I became consumed by dread, noticing all the flaws that made others seem so much greater than I.

Maybe I was lucky today. The weather seemed ideal: the sun was not too bright, the breeze was not too strong, and the heat was not too intense. Now there was no mirror; I felt good. I avoided looking into any windows, fearing I might see my reflection. Maybe if I thought I looked handsome, I would honestly believe it. I walked quickly, fearing I would be late, even though I had five minutes to spare.

My stomach fluttered, and I felt as if I were walking with a limp – every passerby I glimpsed, I felt, was staring at me. My muscles twitched as I pulled out my phone to check the time. There was still plenty of time, yet I picked up the pace.

Alina stood on the corner where we arranged to meet. She, too, was early. A white coat, verging on grey, hugged her torso, paired with jeans that were neither too baggy nor too slim on her legs. Her black hair was straightened and lay glossy above her shoulders. A few strands awkwardly pushed their way in front of her eyes, and she flicked them out of the way.

Her face lit up when she saw me, waving like I might have missed her if she didn't. Seeing her excited to see me gobbled my nerves and replaced them with excitement. But I don't think I showed it as much as she did.

'So we're gonna get coffee first?' she asked.

'Yeah, you like coffee? I know a nice little cafe. I go there quite often alone.'

'I *love* coffee. You know, I worked as a barista before the restaurant.'

Her deep wood-brown eyes widened. There it was, her raw, unfiltered happiness. I liked that about her. Her happiness had no other meaning; it was never forced. She was only happy when she was truly happy. It wasn't like Hadi's happiness, which always carried a tinge of something unnatural.

What would it be like to live with such pure, beautiful emotions?

'I didn't know. So why'd you quit? You prefer bartending?'

She sighed. 'Honestly, I'd rather be a barista. I love coffee. I find it interesting. It's much more calming than alcohol. But baristas get paid less. You know what *really* pisses me off?'

I couldn't help but chuckle. Her emotions were so interesting. She switched from happiness to annoyance, but she spoke with such passion that it was addictive to listen to. It made me forget anything I was thinking about and focus only on her.

'What?'

'People who complain about the price of coffee. Like, I get it, it's not cheap. But I worked for an independent speciality coffee shop. Our coffee was cheaper than the bigger chains', and *so* much better; yet, people *still* complained. Like they thought they were entitled to cheap, good-tasting coffee. It's a long process to make coffee. Baristas are only a small part. A cup of coffee contains the whole world, yet people think they're entitled to get it for cheap.'

She took a breath and shook her head.

'And you know what, it's always the rich people. Like people wearing nice clothes and expensive watches, you know the type. They have the money to spend on a cup of coffee, yet they're the ones who feel like they should pay less. It makes me sick.'

Why was I smiling? I liked coffee, but I didn't relate to it on the same level as Alina. She talked about it with such passion that I couldn't help but feel a slight tug of admiration.

Her face caught a brush stroke of red. 'Sorry. I didn't mean to go off like that.'

I put my hands up. 'No, no, please talk more. I find it interesting. Plus, I agree. We work for just above minimum wage. If we can pay for coffee, the ones earning triple our pay can pay for it, too.'

She chuckled. 'I always thought you were a genius.'

That sentence almost made me throw up. Not in a bad way. But in a good way.

We talked about coffee for the entire walk to the cafe. It was on the quieter side of the city, so I preferred it a lot more than the ones plopped down in the middle of the chaos. Although there were fewer people on the streets, the shop remained popular.

A gentle scent of freshly roasted coffee and pastries drifted from the open windows. I smelled it from two buildings down. On the outside of the building, *Akari Coffee* was written in brown letters.

Alina stopped walking and stared at me before entering the cafe. 'Did you know?'

'Know what?'

'This is where I worked.'

'Oh, is it okay if we go in? There's more around here if you wanna go to another—'

Before I could finish the sentence, she entered the coffee shop. I tried to hold the door open for her like Hadi said to, but it didn't appear like she would've cared if I slammed it in her face or opened the window for her to crawl through as long as she got in somehow.

'I've only been here twice since I left,' she said, in a slightly hushed voice as if scared people might hear her. 'I quit four years ago.'

'Are you sure it's okay? We can go somewhere else if you'd like.'

'No, no, it's fine. It's just weird being back.' She glanced around. 'Being a bartender pays better than a barista, so . . .'

I ordered a cortado, and she ordered a pour-over with some single-origin beans from a country I had never heard of. We sat in the corner, putting a slight distance between us and the other people. The cafe had an old wooden interior with heavy wooden tables. It was slightly dark, with rustic lighting. People chattered whilst baristas rushed about behind the bar. Jazz hummed through the speakers. There was a line for takeaway orders, but few people sat inside. I often came to this cafe to read. It was spacious and relaxing.

Alina didn't speak much whilst we waited for the coffee, and I didn't make much of an attempt at conversation.

She stared behind the bar at the baristas, watching their every move, whilst inserting comments about their techniques. I didn't want to interrupt her, so I sat quietly and watched with her. The staff all wore black, slightly baggy jeans and white shirts. Their shirts remained loose and were surprisingly spotless. How they could work with a brown liquid without getting it smudged on them was a mystery to me.

'When I was a barista, I didn't like it when customers watched me,' she said, not taking her eyes away from the bar, but she glanced away when a barista looked up, as if she was scared of being caught. 'But, now I think, being a barista isn't only making coffee, it's also entertaining the people who drink the coffee.'

'Do you know any of these people?'

'Only one. The rest have left. But it doesn't look like she's working today.' She paused and looked at me. 'Look,' she said, nodding towards the bar. 'Notice it's busy. But the baristas aren't cutting steps. They're not rushing. They truly care about their craft. They're good baristas.'

'But of course you're better.'

She looked away from the bar and broke into a smile. As if awoken from a trance. 'Well, of course. I do miss it. Working in coffee. I like bartending, but there was just something about making coffee that was so' – she paused as if searching for a word – 'pleasant.'

A few minutes later, a young woman came to our table, holding our drinks. With black bags under her eyes, she looked far too tired for a girl her age. A wavy smile flashed on her face – a customer service smile, not a genuine smile. I'd seen her working many times, and she seemed to enjoy it, but she was always tired and never showed unfiltered joy. I wondered what her life was like outside of work. Did she still live with her parents? Did she have many friends? Perhaps she was still a student.

Sometimes I felt bad coming here. It was because of me that they had to make an extra drink and do extra work. If I didn't come so often, maybe they'd get a free two-minute break to catch up with other drinks or have a breather. I could easily make coffee in my apartment, so I wouldn't force them to do more work. Yet, I still came here, and I enjoyed my time here more than I would sitting in my apartment drinking coffee. So, did a stranger's futile grab at peace make it okay to force them to do extra work?

We thanked her for the coffee, and Alina added in an extra comment about how delicious it looked to her.

A heart was painted on my cortado, and it made me smile. It was served in a small, grey porcelain cup. We toasted and then sipped. The first sip of coffee felt like easing into a warm bath. Blackberry, stone fruit, and treacle melting onto my tongue. Truthfully, I didn't know as much as Alina, but as long as I appreciated the taste, I think that's what counted.

Her eyes widened, a smile slowly crawling onto her lips. 'It's good.'

'So how was it?'

I sat on the metal counter inside the restaurant's kitchen as Hadi finished his tasks. Like every day, we were the last two closing. He had his portable speaker on the counter, punk music blaring out of it, just sitting on the border of being too loud.

He bobbed his head as he finished mopping the last section of the floor, splashing the soapy, chemical-scented water everywhere.

'It was good,' I shouted over the music.

He grabbed his phone and lowered the volume. '*It was good.* Just that? Tell me everything.'

I walked through the events. It didn't go exactly to plan. I went off course a little, not on purpose. We never made it to the art gallery. Time flew so fast that I didn't realise time was passing at first. We sat in the coffee shop for a couple of hours, talking slowly. We talked about nothing particularly interesting, but I remembered feeling relaxed. Not often did I feel relaxed. I noticed how long we'd been in there after I saw the inside of my cup was dry; we'd finished our drinks a while ago, but it didn't seem to matter.

Afterwards, I suggested we go on a walk at the nearby park. It was a beautiful park, and the season was right for it. The autumn leaves fell gracefully in their pure colours. We walked for a few hours, grabbed some food, and ate it on a park bench.

Before I knew it, the day came to an end. I walked her to the metro station, waved goodbye, and then walked to my apartment. At the end of the day, I didn't feel anything. Should I have felt happy that it went well? But the only thing I had felt was a slight hunger. When I recalled the events, a slight tinge of hope for the future began to blossom.

After I finished telling what happened, Hadi asked, 'Did you kiss her?'

'What?'

'Did you?'

'No. I mean, it's like the first date. You don't kiss on the first date. I mean, right?'

'That's okay. Did you hug her goodbye?'

I swallowed. I didn't do any of those things. It never even occurred to me what I should have done. Did I do something wrong? *What is right and wrong in that situation?* It wouldn't have felt natural if I tried. But I didn't even think of that, so how would I know if it would have felt natural?

Hadi shrugged. 'Don't sweat it, man. Take it slow.'

'But we're meeting again next Tuesday. This time we're gonna go to the gallery.'

'Good idea.' Hadi stretched. 'All finished! Wanna grab a couple drinks before heading back?'

Hadi was always the first to ask me. Not once had I invited him for a drink after work. Maybe next time I would ask.

As we walked to the pub, Hadi sprang a question on me. It was a normal question, but for some reason, it made me feel sick.

'You have been on a date before, right?' Hadi said. 'I've known you for six years, but you've never been on a date in that time, right?'

I couldn't reply. I knew the answer. Was it normal for a twenty-seven-year-old man to have never been on a date? I searched my memory. Surely there was a time I'd been on a date. But I searched deep, and there was nothing.

Hadi waited for a bit, but I didn't reply.

'You've done *it*, right?'

It was like someone had wrapped their hand around my organs, squeezing them, pulling at them. That was the first time I really thought about it. It had crossed my mind, but there was never an opportunity when I could've done it. I was twenty-seven years old and still a virgin. Shame engulfed me.

Hadi laughed to ease the tension. 'Don't worry, bro. That's a good thing. Honest!'

I couldn't say a word. I always thought I had time. After all, that's what everyone told me. But now there I was, a twenty-seven-year-old with no experience. I would need to have sex one day, but now all I could think about was how painfully awkward it would be when it came to that time.

'I don't feel well. I think I'll go home today.'

Hadi's shoulders dropped. 'Sure thing, man.'

We walked to the metro station together. Normally, I'd walk back; it was only a twenty-minute walk, but my energy had vanished. We made it in time to catch the last train.

On the train, Hadi whispered to me so nobody else could hear. 'I had a friend who lost his at thirty. He's married now and happier than anyone I know. Don't sweat it.' After a pause, he said with a slightly serious face, 'If this were the sixth century, you'd be sacrificed to please the gods. *The blood of a twenty-seven-year-old virgin.*'

Chapter 4
ART

Not many things brought me joy. Art was one of the few things that did. Since my first breath, I wanted to be an artist.

Art spoke to me in ways humans weren't capable of, caressing the deepest parts of my soul. Embracing the parts that needed to be seen. On my days off, I'd wander around galleries aimlessly. It was the only time when I'd feel something worth feeling.

But I was never too fond of my art. I could never express all that I wanted to. A barrier stood between me and the brush, and I couldn't break it down. I dreamed of having one of my paintings in a renowned gallery. But even if I did, it wouldn't bring me joy. Only suffering, knowing that I didn't paint what I truly wanted to paint, just a poor imitation of it.

When I was working, my mind often wandered to art. Once, a customer asked me a question, and I was so far off in my own world that I replied with *midnight blue*. It was a question about wine, but I was thinking about the colours used in a painting I'd seen the day before. After that, all I could think about was crawling into a hole and not coming up until that person had grown old and died. That way, I'd never need to think of that moment again.

Everything led to embarrassment, one way or another. Sometimes it wouldn't affect me, other times it made me want to split my stomach open and rid myself of everything disgusting. Sometimes I thought the only thing that stopped me from killing myself was the embarrassment I'd feel afterwards. What might people say after I had done it? How they would talk about me. I would be dead, so would it matter what people said about me? Yes, it would.

I don't know why I often felt that way. I don't think I'd had any traumatic experiences it could have stemmed from. Maybe it was just the terror of standing out. Or maybe it was something I was born with. Did everyone feel the same way I did? If I thought about it like that, then it didn't feel as bad. People were wrapped up in their own worlds, so why should they pay attention to me? Believing this made me feel a little better.

Four things excited me in life. Closing the restaurant and speaking with Hadi. Wandering around art galleries. Art. And the next time I'd see Alina.

Those were my motivators.

I woke early on Tuesday morning. This time we were going to a coffee shop that Alina had recommended.

I brushed my teeth, ate breakfast, took a dump, showered, put on clothes, and brushed my teeth once more before leaving. A routine perfect for starting a good day.

This time, Alina was late. I got there five minutes early and waited awkwardly outside the metro station. Strangers' gazes penetrated me as they walked past. Sometimes I checked my phone to act as if I were busy. I didn't mind waiting. People get late, and that's okay. There were many reasons why she might be late.

But still, a thought crept into my mind. Was she not coming? Was it an excuse to get out of seeing me?

I guessed that would be fine. She had no reason to come. Of course, I wanted to see her, but if she didn't want to see me, that couldn't be helped.

Fifteen minutes had passed, and a message popped up on my phone.

Getting off the train now! Sorry!

I smiled slightly. She was coming. I checked my reflection on my phone screen, brushing at the top of my hair with my palm, forcing the wretched curls to flatten. I put the phone down before I could notice my other flaws.

She came out of the metro's exit, breathing slightly heavily. 'I'm so sorry! I forgot something, so I had to go back to get it, that's why I'm late.'

'Me, too . . . I mean, don't worry. I was a little bit late, too,' I lied, trying to put her at ease.

'Oh, that's good then. You didn't wait long?'

'Not at all.'

We walked together to her choice of coffee shop, and it was delicious. It was a Chinese-inspired speciality coffee shop. Serving a selection of pour-overs, espresso-based drinks, and multiple signature drinks. On the walk there, Alina talked for ten minutes about the barista who had won multiple competitions, who worked there. And once we arrived, instead of talking to the barista, she kept stealing glances at her as she created drinks.

We sat there enjoying each other's company; we talked, and sometimes we didn't talk. I found those were the best people to be with. Those with whom we could sit in silence, and you didn't need to talk to be understood.

Alina was an easy person to work with. She had a passion for her job that few people shared. She was easy to be around, and I felt at ease when I was with her. When she stood beside me, I forgot so many insecurities that often bothered me.

After coffee, we walked to the gallery. I had been to almost every gallery in the city, but this one had escaped me. It was on the second floor of a building, with only one sign advertising it. It had only two reviews online and only held exhibitions for small artists.

We went into the building. It had four floors. They were all apartments, apart from the floor with the gallery. It was a shady, grey building, but once we reached the gallery, it opened to a spacious room with long white walls. Only one woman sat at the reception, typing away on a laptop. She paid no attention to us when we walked into the main gallery.

'Do we not need to pay?' Alina asked.

'Nah, this one's free,' I said, whilst slipping a five-pound note into a donations jar.

Only one artist, Hedro Francis, was having an exhibition this month. He was nowhere to be seen. Although the artists sometimes attended their exhibitions, they couldn't be expected to come every day, especially since it was a month-long event.

The gallery was empty except for us. Small and large paintings clung to the walls. From the second I entered, a fire brewed inside of me. I didn't know what it was or where it came from, but it was there.

I went from painting to painting, with Alina following behind. Sometimes she'd comment about something she liked, or sometimes she'd simply admire them, or sometimes she'd stare at me whilst I analysed the paintings. First, I examined it from afar, then I took a step closer to see the finer details. Lastly, I assessed how the painting made me feel. Did I feel happy? Sad? Anything at all?

'Have you ever been to France?' Alina asked, staring at a painting of three young men sitting in a field. For some reason, they had a ladder, and one was sitting on that. They were idle, staring at nothing.

'Once, when I was young. We went to Paris for a family holiday.'

'You're lucky. Was it good? I've never been.' She took a step closer to the painting. 'I think they have a lot of good art in Paris. Let's go together sometime.'

I laughed, sure she was joking. 'Y-yeah, let's do that.'

My chest got heavier as I walked through the gallery. I wasn't sure why, but these paintings were making me awfully sad. Absolutely wretched. It was no mood to share with another. That's why I enjoyed visiting galleries alone. The emotions I felt weren't meant to be shared.

At the end of the white rooms was a singular room, slightly smaller than the rest. The gallery we'd walked through so far contained multiple paintings, but this one contained only one. Unlike the others, it was not hung in the middle of the wall but instead stuck onto the bottom of the wall. I guessed it was an artistic decision, the way the artist wanted us to view his piece. At first glance, it appeared to be a slightly distorted portrait.

I stared at it and did my usual routine. Brush strokes, colours, shades, absorbing it all. I took a few steps back to admire it all. Admiring its unique use of lines and colours. Without knowing why, I began to cry. I hadn't cried for a long time. Perhaps not for a couple of months. I remembered the last time, it was out of frustration, not sadness.

But these were pure melancholic tears sliding down my face. I made no noise, allowing the tears to tickle my cheeks. Alina stood next to me. She made no comment as I wept, instead gently taking my hand in hers.

I looked at her, then back at the painting and said, 'This man is incredibly sad.'

She was silent for a few seconds, perhaps collecting her thoughts. Not many knew how to react when a grown man broke down and cried.

'Who?' she finally said.

'Hedro Francis. This artist.'

I could see it in the colours he used and the way he had caressed the canvas with his brushes. Lines he had scribbled onto the world. Fears he had vomited onto that canvas. It was all there, in its raw, disgusting beauty, for the eye to witness. What he'd painted had little to do with the art itself. It lay far deeper within.

This artist will kill himself, I thought. I had never been so certain of anything. If he hadn't already, he would eventually kill himself. He was tortured by life, and he translated that into his paintings. Hedro Francis lived a miserable life. I wished I could have hugged him, pushed my hands through his art, and held him gently. One tortured soul holding another. Tell him it would be okay even if it were a lie. A soul needed a few lies to comfort the pain. Without sweet, innocent lies, one would be driven to a state like that. One would eventually be tortured out of life.

I began to sob. My life didn't seem as bad now. No matter what, I could never imagine myself falling into such misery as Hedro endured.

I had never pitied a creature. Things happened, and what happened, happened. It couldn't be avoided. But this was the first time I had ever wanted to help someone. I wanted to save this man. Nobody should be forced to suffer and be tormented to this level. It was disgusting.

Alina gently wrapped her arms around my neck, in slow movements, as if she were approaching a wild deer.

I lifted my arms and held her waist, my sobs shrinking to breaths, and then the tears stopped, leaving my face blotchy and my eyes bloodshot.

'I'm sorry,' I croaked.

Her arms tightened around me. 'What for?'

I let go of her, and then she unwrapped from me. I didn't say anything, I didn't need to. I looked at her, and she understood.

'You're allowed to show emotion.'

I turned back to the painting, to bid this morbid soul goodbye.

'I don't understand art like you.' She pushed a strand of her hair aside. 'But I think it's beautiful how it can make us feel so deeply. I want to learn more.'

As we walked out of the gallery, a thought came to me. That was the first time I had done something utterly embarrassing. The only emotion I should have felt was embarrassment, but for some odd reason, I felt nothing but calm. I was a grown man who broke down crying in an empty art gallery.

The painting still weighed on me, and I couldn't stop thinking about that artist, but that was deeper inside of me. At that moment, the only thing that mattered was that I was still alive, and I had my whole life ahead of me. I wasn't like Hedro. My life wasn't that miserable, and I wasn't going to take it from myself.

From this point on, I would live.

Chapter 5
CRY

L IFE BECAME A ROUTINE. I'D WORK, DRINK, AND TALK WITH Hadi, and on Tuesdays, I'd meet Alina. I wasn't entirely sure, but maybe I was becoming happy. I no longer had to force a customer service smile on people when they entered the restaurant. I smiled because I wanted to. I smiled because I was happy to see happy people.

Life still weighed heavily on my soul. Fears for the future still clouded my judgement, sometimes, to the point where it made me want to do nothing at all. Before, I would do nothing, but now I had made promises that forced me to move.

I went back to that gallery alone a few weeks later. A few days earlier, the exhibition had changed to another one. The gallery was empty again – only the same woman at the reception, who, again, paid me no attention when I walked in. When I walked out, I thanked her, and she looked at me with such woeful eyes and smiled. It couldn't be easy to work surrounded by such devastating art. If I were her, I think I'd kill myself at that desk after four days. I wouldn't be able to live surrounded by art from such a sorrowful soul. Digging into my brain every second I took my eyes away from the wall.

After I got home, I searched for Hedro Francis's name. I typed his name into my phone as if I were searching for a dirty fetish. I glanced around my empty apartment as if someone might be watching me. I sat on the edge of my creaky bed, phone in hand, and pressed search.

He was alive. I had to refresh the page to check I hadn't misread it, but there was nothing about his death. There were many articles about his art, so I decided to lie down and read.

They spoke nothing about the lines dripping in woe or the melancholic colours screaming for help. The reviewers spoke only of the beauty in his art and the use of colours and lines to amplify this and that.

Nobody cared. Nobody could see this artist's pain. All they saw was his greatness.

I didn't deny his greatness. His art was phenomenal, but it was there, in its raw beauty, that this artist was experiencing a life of dejection. Why did nobody comment on that?

A few weeks later, I searched for Hedro Francis again. He had killed himself two weeks before.

I never knew the man, yet I cried for him. Perhaps I was crying because I was glad that he could finally have a taste of peace. Now, his soul could rest. Hedro Francis was thirty-nine years old at the time of his death. He had two children and had been married for ten years.

The more I read about his life, the less bad it seemed. He couldn't make enough money selling his art, so he ran a fresh fruit and vegetable store with his wife. He was a popular man in his community, loved by all. His wife and family spoke of the shock.

He was a happy man. Never stopped laughing, they said.

I was shocked. I wish he had spoken to me.

That line stood out to me. He *had* spoken to you.

'It was all in his art, but you were too blind to see it,' I said, as if his wife were in the room with me.

That night, I painted my greatest painting. For hours, I leant over a canvas, with brushes soaking in an empty jam jar I had filled with water. Acrylic paint splashed all over my grey overalls and desk. The white sheet I had laid on the floor was stained with paint that had escaped my brush. It was a gruesome yet beautiful sight.

I wiped my face, removing the sweat and layering it with paint instead. After I felt I could add no more, I went straight to the fridge and downed a bottle of water.

To me, it was a village with red-brick buildings, lush green grass, and villagers dressed in green, with red flowers tied around their heads. It may have appeared as splashes on a canvas to any other human. Twisted lines, vile colours, and brush strokes screaming to be seen. Even if only one person saw this canvas and understood, that's all that mattered.

I wanted to be understood, but I didn't need to be. Understanding is rare and fleeting. To be seen by the right person at the right time was infinity on high.

For a second after I put the brush down, I understood myself. It was short-lived, but it was the first time.

I slept well that night.

'You look different.' Hadi held his head in his hands as he leant across the sticky bar table, staring at me.

'Do I?'

'You don't *feel* different?'

'Perhaps? I guess, m-maybe a little.'

A smirk tickled at Hadi's lips. He leant closer and whispered to me, 'So, have you done *it* yet?'

My stomach did a little flip, and I swirled the beer in my cup. It had been three months since we first went to the coffee shop together. We never spoke about what we were. Neither did I know what we were. Were we friends who hung out together? Or were we a couple going on dates once a week? Or were we something in between?

We flirted with each other. Sometimes. But we never took it much further than that. It felt friendly. I liked her,

I did. And Hadi knew that, too, without me needing to say anything to him. He encouraged me to make a move. *She'll lose interest soon,* he said.

Last Tuesday, I finally did.

Before I saw her, I felt compelled to do or say something. We had lunch together first. There was a restaurant I had been wanting to go to, and I asked if she'd like to go with me. The food was fantastic. It was a casual Mediterranean restaurant. After eating, I suggested we take a walk around the park. So, that's what we did. In the park, I was sick to my stomach, and all I could think about was when and how I would say or do something. There never seemed to be a right time. I had pictured how it would go in my head. Perhaps, we'd go to a quiet area in the park, I'd make her laugh, and when we were relaxed and at ease, I'd slowly lean in to kiss her.

But that's not what happened. It was getting late, so we started heading back. The sun began her descent, so whilst we still had light, I decided to adjust our way back to walk through the flower garden. It was a beautiful part of the park. The gardeners changed the flowers every season, according to what thrived at that temperature. This time, there were blue flowers. I knew little about flowers, so I couldn't tell the names. But I knew they were beautiful and made me feel warm. Rows of trees stood among the flowers. It was a secluded area of the park, so few people came here, apart from those who enjoyed flowers and appreciated the effort that went into creating such displays. Their scent was fresh, floral, and slightly sweet, but not overpowering.

I crouched to get a closer look at them.

'You like flowers?' she asked.

'Everybody likes flowers. Unless, well, people who're allergic to them. But I guess they like how they look, at least, r-right?'

I stood and didn't realise how close she was to me. Her eyes were slightly wider than usual. Her lips quivered as if forcing down a smile. I looked at her eyes, then down at her lips, and back to her eyes. My heart was racing; I felt as if I was going to pass out. I dug my toes into the ground to stop my hands from shaking. My breath was uneven. I looked at her lips for maybe a second too long, because this time her smile appeared.

Fuck it. I began to lean in. I closed my eyes. But at the last microsecond, I pulled back. 'C-can I kiss you?'

The words came out in a pathetic slur. Everything caved inside of me; I felt as if I were turning into a black hole. I regretted saying anything; I should have committed to it. Instantly, my body became spiky, as sweat forced its way out. As my mind raced, she broke into a larger smile and nodded.

So then, I did it. I kissed her. I was twenty-seven years old and had just had my first kiss. It didn't last long. I pulled back, and she smiled, then I smiled, and we both laughed.

'We can practise,' she said to me.

That was one of those rare moments of pure, unfiltered happiness.

I can't remember what it felt like physically. The rush consumed me entirely.

I stared into my beer, smiling slightly. 'I kissed her.'

Hadi was silent, staring at me, his mouth slightly parted. I couldn't read his expression. Maybe he was disappointed in me for taking so long. 'For the first time?'

'Yeah.'

'And what did she say?'

'"We can practise."'

Hadi's mouth stretched into a smile. A pure, undiluted smile. A laugh erupted from his mouth, so loud that others glanced at us. Blood rushed to my face. He stretched his hand across the table, took mine, and shook it.

'That's my boy,' he roared. 'I've never been so proud of anyone.'

A laugh erupted from me, too. I tried to drink the last few drops of my beer, but ended up choking on it and spitting it back into the glass. I laughed harder, and so did Hadi.

As the laughs died down, I noticed others glancing at us, and once Hadi noticed, too, an uncontrollable fit of giggles consumed us.

I wanted to tell him how I felt, how violently terrified I was, and that at the age of twenty-seven, I had my first kiss. I wanted to thank him for being my friend and listening to me.

These last few weeks, I'd been drowning in joy. This was what it meant to live life. I wanted to laugh every day, so hard that I forgot to breathe.

Once we stopped laughing, Hadi went to the bar to order another two beers for us. I rested my arm on the sticky table and put my cheek in my palm. My eyes started to droop slightly. Work was tough today. Customers had been polite, but they wanted everything explained to them as if they were toddlers; they wanted to know all the ingredients used and their origins. I didn't mind explaining it to them, but I had other tables to serve, too. Customers prioritised themselves.

I chose to leave that at work. Right now, I was enjoying myself. I didn't need a negative thought to spoil that. I was allowed to be happy.

Hadi returned with two beers and handed one to me. I cupped the icy glass in my hands and stared at Hadi. His smile slowly faded.

'I want to ask you something,' he said.

'Sure.'

'I want you to be my best man.' He paused, then continued, 'I've thought about it and talked to Ri about it. You're my best friend. I want you to be my best man. Will you?'

My smile stepped away, and my mouth parted. Without any sign of prewarning, tears erupted from my eyes. In the middle of the pub, I, a twenty-seven-year-old man, began to cry. I cried because I had a best friend, and I cried because he wanted me to be his best man.

Chapter 6
I'M NOT A NUDIST

Hadi died four months before his wedding. Four days before, he had asked me to be his best man. After work, we went for a drink like usual. Hadi took the metro back, and I decided to walk. I lived one stop away, and the metro shaved off only five minutes, so I rarely used it.

The witnesses said he tripped and fell onto the tracks. He had always stood dangerously close to the platform edge, and whenever I questioned why he did it, he would reply with, *So I'm the first on.* He'd say it in such a charming way that it never made anyone question it.

I didn't leave my apartment for two weeks. The restaurant was closed for a week before they could find staff to cover us. The boss allowed me to take a month off. I didn't shower for a week. I ordered food to my apartment, but found no enjoyment in putting fuel into my body. I ate because, without food, I felt sick, and I didn't eat because I felt sick.

I didn't message Alina for all that time. She messaged me, and I read them, but I couldn't find the energy to reply. I admit that sometimes I was jealous of Hadi, but that jealousy fuelled me. I hoped to be someone like him, and that hope kept me going. Without Hadi, I had no one to be jealous of, no one to strive to be like.

People spoke of their regrets, and when I thought of mine, I could only think of one. Every day after Hadi's death, I wished I had stopped being secretly jealous of him and instead endeavoured to improve myself alongside him.

I missed him. He was truly my greatest friend, if only I had realised that earlier.

I didn't cry. I was numb, feeling only a profound sense of despair.

Hadi was about to get married. He would've had children and created a beautiful family. He could've become a chef at one of the greatest restaurants, with Ri at his side.

Instead, he was splattered on the train tracks.

In the second week, I left. I shaved and showered, then left my apartment. I walked and walked. I had nowhere to go, but I walked. Mindlessly. Aimlessly. Maybe if I walked far enough, I'd forget everything, and I'd start feeling things again. I paid no attention to how I looked or how I smelled. All external elements no longer existed to me. I was a phantom of a man, lifeless, emotionless, gliding to nowhere.

A coldness came from my stomach and expanded to my fingertips. Unknowingly, I walked to the flower gardens, which I had once come to with Alina. The flowers that once sat there before had been replaced with roses. Red roses, poking their heads above their green leaves.

Their sweet aroma drifted into my nose, and I cried into that bed of roses in a public park. For my dead friend, I cried.

Ri came to my apartment a few days later. She had bags under her eyes, but that was the only sign of grief she showed. Ri wasn't a woman who would make you do a double-take. You'd miss her at first glance. She walked as everyone else walked. Breathed as everyone else breathed.

But once you sat down with her, there was something deep in her mind that was pure brilliance. Not many could see that. I could only catch a glimpse of it, like shooting stars that made us realise how big our world was. But Hadi had seen the whole universe. Ri had worked at the restaurant with us; she was a few years older than Hadi and had been his boss. She left a few years ago to work at a better restaurant, and that's when Hadi took her place.

She hugged me tightly. And we cried. I'm not sure how long we stayed in that position. Holding each other and sobbing. But eventually, we parted and she began talking about the funeral.

She had organised a simple funeral, with only his closest family and friends. She saw no point in anything extravagant. I agreed with her.

After we had stopped speaking of morbid things, as she was heading through the door, she said to me, 'He loved you. You were like his brother.'

Then, without another word, she left. She didn't need to say another word, nor did I. For in this situation, words did nothing.

I phoned Alina after Ri left. Having not messaged her since Hadi's death, I needed to apologise. She spoke gently, holding no grudge, and we arranged to see each other.

I cleaned my apartment for the first time since Hadi's death. I opened the balcony door, letting fresh air purify the room. Had I mentioned I had a balcony? Being on the fourth floor, I had privacy from those walking below, so I often sat out there with a book and a cup of coffee. Sometimes, a pencil and a sketchbook. Most of the time, I sat out there naked. I wasn't a nudist, or anything like that. The balcony was completely private, so I didn't need to worry about flashing my neighbours or fellow citizens. It was cleansing to sit outside, naked, with fresh air brushing against my body.

After I'd cleaned my apartment, I got naked and sat down on a small, smooth wooden chair, with a palette, paint, brushes, a jam jar full of water, and a heart full of grief.

On an A3-sized canvas, I began spreading paint, letting my imagination be my inspiration. At first, I didn't know what I was going to paint. Halfway through, I realised I was painting myself. A naked man sat on a balcony with brushes in his hands, a pencil behind his ear, colours poisoning his skin. Once this realisation hit, I committed to it.

I hadn't been a fan of self-portraits. I had no interest in drawing a boring subject. So, I rarely painted them. But as I sat there, with a cold breeze caressing my entire body, and painting the fine details of my well-kept pubic hair, it came to me that this was the first time since my best friend had died that I felt at peace.

I hung the painting on my wall, among all my others, in my worn-out apartment. For a second, I saw potential in the naked man painting on a balcony.

It had been over a month since I last saw Alina. Next week, I was supposed to return to work, and I was dreading it. Dreading being back in the building where I had spent so many hours with my best friend.

I sat on my couch with my hair damp from a shower, and my skin slightly sticky from moisturiser. It wasn't long until Alina knocked on my apartment door. I jumped up, checked my reflection in the mirror before answering it.

She stood there, wearing black jeans and a slightly oversized blue shirt over a white top. Her hair was a shade brighter than when I had last seen her. My heart fluttered, and I couldn't stop staring at her.

'Hi,' she said.

I glanced away. 'Do you want to come in? I can make you some coffee before we head out.'

We had arranged to go on a walk at a nearby park. To catch up after not seeing each other.

'Only if it's good coffee.'

She walked in, and I shut the door behind her. She began looking at the paintings hanging on my walls. I had a little studio apartment. It was minimalistic, apart from the eighty paintings and sketches lazily clinging to my walls. Most of which were mine. Some were from other lesser known artists. I took inspiration from others' art, tucked between my own.

'Are these yours?' Alina asked, without peeling her eyes off the sketches.

'Most of them are.'

'Holy shit.' She spun around and stared at me, her eyes wide. 'Nodo, you're insane. Like this is incredible. It's like a gallery.'

My face got hot. 'It's not much.'

'You're kidding. It's incredible.'

As Alina looked around, I began brewing the coffee. I had bought a small bag of Chinese coffee with a wine yeast fermentation process. It sounded interesting, so I got it. I thought Alina might enjoy it, too. With a hand grinder, I ground the beans, then dropped them into the dripper, and began pouring water slowly.

'I'm sorry I didn't text you,' I said, not looking up from the dripper.

'I understand.' Alina moved next to me and watched as I poured the water. She placed her hand under the kettle. 'Pour a little higher. You'll agitate the grounds better this way.'

I followed her directions as she picked up the bag of beans.

'These sound good. I'm excited.'

I poured the coffee equally between two white ceramic cups, and we sat on my little sofa and drank. My eyes widened as the warm liquid coated my mouth. Flavours of lychee tickled my cheeks. It was such a profound flavour that if I hadn't brewed this coffee and seen the beans, I would've believed it was some strange, brown lychee juice.

Alina laughed after she swallowed. 'Damn, this is a good brew. Is this a new hobby of yours?'

'Newish. I've never brewed coffee to this extent.'

'So, why'd you start now?'

'I was fed up with drinking trash at home.' I glanced at her. 'And you inspired me.'

A giggle escaped her. 'Really? I inspired you? Well, I'm glad.'

She stood, coffee in hand, and walked over to my latest painting. I was forced to look away as she stared at it. Her eyes lingered over certain areas, and a smile grew on her lips.

'Is this you?' she said, without taking her eyes off it.

'Maybe,' I croaked.

I cleared my throat and stared into the coffee cup. That painting was for myself. I hadn't imagined anyone would ever look at it. Perhaps I should have taken it down before Alina came. It didn't cross my mind that she would take an interest in my paintings.

I hardly noticed the art scattered across my walls. It blended into each other, creating a wallpaper that I never took much notice of.

'Why are you naked?' she asked. 'Do you often sit on your balcony naked?'

'Sometimes.'

Laughs erupted from her. 'I have never heard of anyone painting naked on their balcony.'

'Well, I do,' I said, more defensively than I meant to.

'I'm not making fun of you.' Alina smirked. 'There's absolutely nothing wrong with being a nudist. Honestly.'

'I'm not a—'

'I've known nudists before. I'm not judging. But, do you not get complaints from your neighbours?' She lowered her voice. '*He's at it again. That naked man painting on his balcony.*'

The bizarreness of this conversation made a smile creep up on me. 'They can't see me.'

'Are you sure? Do you not feel self-conscious? Being naked outside?'

'Perhaps, it's the only time I don't feel self-conscious.'

Alina laughed harder, sitting down on my bed, clutching her knees. 'That's so ironic.'

Watching Alina uncontrollably laugh over my art made me lose my self-control. I burst out laughing. The whole situation was ridiculous. The more I thought about it, the more I laughed.

'Honestly,' Alina said between laughs, 'that's one of the best paintings I've ever seen. You should get it in a gallery. Hang it up so the world can see it. The world deserves to see it.'

'You think so?'

'I mean, it's deep, right? It is so ridiculous. Like so ridiculous. But it's also deep. It makes me think so much, and that's what good art is! Don't you think so?'

'I guess.'

She stared at me, as if I *guess* wasn't a sufficient answer.

'I mean, yeah. Good art makes us think.'

'Draw me,' she demanded. 'Forget about everything else. I want you to draw me. Draw me, like this will be the last painting you'll ever do.'

I drank the rest of the coffee, stood, and grabbed my sketchbook. Today I was lucky to have such a beautiful subject to paint.

Chapter 7
EXHIBITION

I HAD MY FIRST EXHIBITION AT THE SAME GALLERY WHERE I had seen Hedro's painting. Nearly a year had passed since Hadi's death. I thought about him every day. He inspired me to live, even in his death.

After months of networking, creating portfolios, and pitching them, I had finally landed my own exhibition. I was in the gallery's white rooms, hanging my paintings and sketches on the walls. Alina stood behind me, telling me if it was straight or not.

'How about now?'

'Just a tad more to the left. Stop! That's perfect.'

I hopped down from the ladder and took a few steps back. Then I moved on to the next one, until the gallery was filled with my art.

I hadn't realised how many paintings I had done of Hadi, Alina, and even Ri, until I walked around the gallery, examining my art as if it were another's. I hadn't painted Hadi until after his death. Perhaps, I should have started painting people earlier. It wasn't until I painted myself naked, then painted a portrait of Alina, that I fell in love with painting people.

As Alina and I walked around the gallery, I should have felt sick to the bones, fearing the judgement of my art. However, it was odd, as I felt nothing but a light sensation. Like I wasn't on the planet. I drifted somewhere far from the mundane world. Nothing felt real to me anymore. I had a hot girlfriend, my art was in a gallery, and I was perhaps experiencing happiness.

I still had days when I wanted to do nothing, when every little thing agitated me. I cried now more than ever. Work was the hardest. We cleaned the restaurant and headed straight home. I often found myself crying, walking back home, thinking about the times I had spent with Hadi. Thoughts of quitting the restaurant often crossed my mind. The place reminded me too much of my best friend. A new start might've been better. Other times, I couldn't even think of quitting. Abandoning the restaurant would mean burying the memories I had made with Hadi in there. Even though I cried many times, I also smiled at those memories. *Was it strange that I now cried more than ever, but I also smiled more?*

I didn't know how long this happiness would last, so I tried to think about it less. Even if happiness was fleeting, I was still experiencing it. Since Hadi's death, I only thought about what I felt at that moment, and right now, I felt pretty damn good.

There wasn't a painting of mine in the gallery's final room. A few months after Hadi's death, I bought Hedro

Francis's painting. I hung it in my apartment, above my bed. Every morning, I looked at it. I had brought Hedro's painting along with me, and hung it in the gallery's final room. It was only fitting that this painting deserved to be in my first exhibition.

Acknowledgements

I'm not sure where Nodo's story came from. In early 2025, I wrote the first draft in three days. I had just returned to the UK after studying in Japan for a year.

I'd be lying if I said my year in Japan didn't inspire parts of this story. The friends I made, the people I spoke to, the places I visited, the scenes I witnessed, and the coffee I drank all played a part in this story. So, for that, I thank everyone I met in Japan, my teachers, my classmates, friends, and people who felt like an extension of my family.

There's always an incredible team of people behind stories. First, I'd like to thank all those who beta-read *Crying Over Flowers*. Thank you, Gionkarlo and Rob D.

Editors are always a vital part of any story, so thank you to Louise Pearce, and the team at A.E. Williams, especially Hamin. I always rely on their knowledge and constant support.

I would like to thank my family and friends for their unwavering support throughout my writing, editing, and publishing process.

As always, I'd like to thank all the writers who came before me. Their words shaped my soul, my voice, and my writing. Thank you to them for inspiring us all to write and create. Never stop writing.

BEN T. CLARKE is the founder of Frozen Moon Press, and the author of the Peter Relish Series. Ben focuses on writing enchanting middle grade and young adult fantasy novels, and the occasional short story.

When Ben isn't writing he can be found reading in quiet cafes or making coffee.

Instagram: @ ben.t.clarke

ABOUT THE PUBLISHER

Frozen Moon Press, founded by Ben T. Clarke in 2023, is an independent publishing house specialising in middle grade and young adult fiction. Every time you open one of our books, we aim to transport you to other worlds. We thank you for reading this story and encourage you to support our authors by leaving an honest online review.

WWW.FROZENMOONPRESS.COM